10

D1088019

Presented to

_____

by_____

on_____

I'm Zoë!

I CAN DO IT MYSELF

Melody Carlson
Illustrated by Elena Kucharik

Tyndale House Publishers, Inc.
WHEATON, ILLINOIS

Visit Tyndale's exciting Web site at www.tyndale.com

Edited by Betty Free Swanberg
Designed by Catherine Bergstrom

Library of Congress Cataloging-in-Publication Data
Carlson, Melody.
    I'm Zoe!: I can do it myself / Melody Carlson ; illustrated by Elena Kucharik.
        p. cm. — (Little blessings)
Summary: Rhyming text and artwork celebrate taking good care of ourselves and our
possessions.
    ISBN 0-8423-7673-9 (alk. paper)
    1. Body, Human—Religious aspects—Christianity—Juvenile literature. 2. Conduct of life—
Juvenile literature. [1. Life skills. 2. Growth. 3. Christian life.] I. Kucharik, Elena, ill. II. Title. III.
Little blessings picture books.
    BT741.3 .C37 2003
    646.7—dc21   2002015173

Printed in Italy

09 08 07 06 05 04 03
7 6 5 4 3 2 1

Thank you for making me so
wonderfully complex! Your workmanship
is marvelous—and how well I know it.

PSALM 139:14

I am Zoë.
　　It's my turn
To tell you what
　　I like to learn.
So come along,
　　and you will see
The ways I take
　　good care of me!

2

4

"Wake-up time!"
  my mommy said.
So I get up
  and make my bed.
It's hard to get
  the pillows right.
They must have flip-flopped
  in the night.

5

I am able
  to get dressed.
I choose the clothes
  I like the best.
But here's the latest
  Zoë news—
I can buckle
  my own shoes!

When I fill up
    my cereal bowl,
Some milk spills out—
    is there a hole?
But even when
    I sort of mess it,
I can ask
    for God to bless it.

I can brush
   my teeth just right—
Go up and down
   to keep them white.

I comb my hair—
    count one, two, three.
I wash my face
    and smile at me.

Even though
    I may look little,
I am learning
    how to fiddle.
I play notes
    like A, B, C
And practice singing
    "Do, re, mi."

Today I learned
   a trick that's new:
I can care
   for others, too!
To feed my goldfish
   is a cinch.
It only takes
   a teeny pinch.

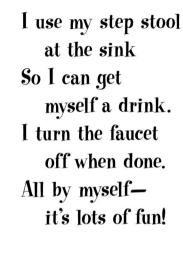

I use my step stool
    at the sink
So I can get
    myself a drink.
I turn the faucet
    off when done.
All by myself—
    it's lots of fun!

Some buttons can be
   hard to do—
'Cause I can't always
   push them through.
That's why I like
   a zipper better;
I can zip my
   new blue sweater!

I'm learning to
    be safe outside
When on a walk
    or when I ride.
I look both ways
    to cross the street.
We hold hands
    and move our feet.

23

I'm also learning
    how to bake—
Cookies aren't
    so hard to make.
I mix the sugar,
    eggs, and butter . . .
Roll out dough
    and use a cutter.

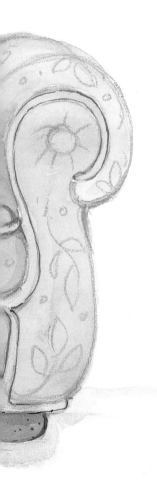

Do you suppose
my friends are home?
Well, I know how
to use the phone.
So I call Kaitlyn.
I call Jack.
And Parker says
he'll call me back.

28

I ask my friends
   to come for tea
To have some cookies
   baked by me.
Then I can serve,
   and I can pour.
And I can say,
   "Do you want more?"

29

I like my toys—
   I like to play.
I like to put them
   all away.
I place my dollies
   in a row.
I stack my games
   and books just so.

I know how
    to plant a seed.
And I know what
    my flowers need.
While I give water,
    God gives sun,
And daisies bloom
    for everyone!

33

My words at dinner
    are all new:
"Please," "You're welcome,"
    and "Thank you."
Good manners seem
    to be worthwhile,
And being kind
    makes others smile!

I'm learning how
   to fill the tub.
Then I get in
   and rub-dub-dub.
I find big bubbles
   everywhere—
And I can even
   wash my hair!

It's time to put
   my jammies on—
Right foot, left foot,
   then I'm done.
I like to read
   my favorite book.
The bookshelf is
   the place to look.

40

Now I must climb
    right into bed.
I know just how
    to bow my head.
I count my blessings—
    one, two, three. . . .
I'm learning to
    take care of me!

About the Author

Melody Carlson has written more than 50 books for children. Awarded the 1999 ECPA Gold Medallion for her children's book *King of the Stable*, she has also appeared on the ECPA best-sellers list with *Benjamin's Box* and *The Prayer of Jabez for Little Ones*, as well as several other titles.

With a degree in early childhood education, Melody taught preschool for many years, enjoying a firsthand relationship with children and books. She also writes for teens and adults.

Melody has two grown sons and currently resides in the mountains of central Oregon, where she enjoys biking, hiking, and camping with her husband, Christopher, and dog, Bailey.

About the Illustrator

Elena Kucharik, well-known Care Bears artist, has created the Little Blessings characters, which appear in a line of Little Blessings products for young children and their families.

Born in Cleveland, Ohio, Elena received a bachelor of fine arts degree in commercial art at Kent State University. After graduation she worked as a greeting card artist and art director at American Greetings Corporation in Cleveland.

For the past 25 years Elena has been a freelance illustrator. During this time she was the lead artist and developer of Care Bears, as well as a designer and illustrator for major corporations and publishers. For the last 10 years Elena has been focusing her talents on illustrations for children's books.

Elena and her husband live in Madison, Connecticut, and have two grown daughters.

Products in the Little Blessings line

Bible for Little Hearts
Prayers for Little Hearts
Promises for Little Hearts
Lullabies for Little Hearts
Lullabies Cassette

Blessings Everywhere
Rain or Shine
God Makes Nighttime Too
Birthday Blessings
Christmas Blessings
God Loves You
Thank You, God!
ABC's
Count Your Blessings
Blessings Come in Shapes
Many-Colored Blessings

What Is God Like?
Who Is Jesus?
What about Heaven?
Are Angels Real?
What Is Prayer?

I'm Kaitlyn!
I'm Zoë!
I'm Jack!
I'm Parker!

Little Blessings New Testament
  & Psalms

Blessings Every Day
Questions from Little Hearts

God Created Me!
    A memory book of baby's first year